The world's best mum is:

....

With love from:

....

To my mum, with love, T.K.
For Mum and Dad, and everything you do, J.L.

First published in 2013 by Hodder Children's Books
This paperback edition first published in 2014

Hodder Children's Books, 338 Euston Road, London, NW1 3BH
Hodder Children's Books Australia, Level 17/207 Kent Street, Sydney, NSW 2000

The right of Timothy Knapman to be identified as the author and Jamie Littler as the illustrator
of this Work has been asserted by them in accordance with the Copyright, Designs and Patents Act 1988.

A catalogue record of this book is available from the British Library.

ISBN: 978 1 444 90817 6

Hodder Children's Books is a division of Hachette Children's Books
An Hachette UK Company
www.hachette.co.uk

Mum's the Word

TIMOTHY KNAPMAN and JAMIE LITTLER

Hodder
Children's
Books

A division of Hachette Children's Books

What's the word that feels like a **cuddle?** Like splashing and sploshing through a great big **puddle?**

A word like a **party**
when your friends all come?

I can't think,
my head's gone numb!

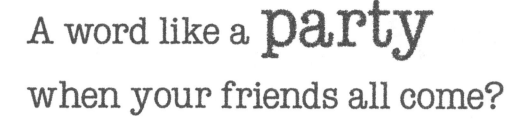

It's a word as warm as a **goodnight kiss.**

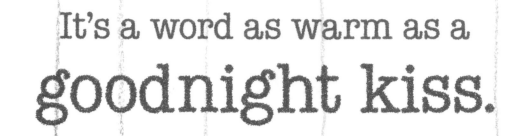

There's no other word
that's as good as this.

It's a word like your favourite
bedtime story.

It's a word
that tastes like a
Knickerbocker
Glory.

It's a word like **ice cream** on a summer's day.

A word like the **park**

where you love to play.

Like the **perfect present** on Christmas Day.

Oh, what's the word
I'm trying to say?

It lifts you up like a
great balloon.

And when you're ill, it means,
"Get well soon!"

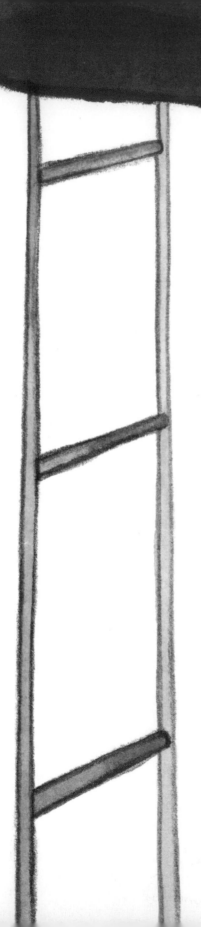

It's a word that says,
"I love you so,"

And, "Let's have fun!
Away we go!"

It's a word like the
dearest wish you make

When you're blowing
out the candles on your
birthday cake!

It's a word
like the SUN,
it's warm and bright.
Like a firework,
it lights up the
night.

And when you're out in
the dark and rain

And you just can't wait
to get **home** again.

When your own front
door will open wide,

It's the word that keeps

you **WARM** inside.

It's a word like a

song you love to hum,

That cheers you up
when you're feeling glum.

A word that feels like a
tickle on
the tum...

I know the word! The word is...

... "Mum!"